The Gardens

The Bedchambers

The Great Hall

The Armory

The Kitchen

The Tournament Field

For
Tom and Ben

With thanks to Sally

Copyright © 1998 by Deri and Jim Robins
All rights reserved. First U.S. edition 1998
Library of Congress Cataloging-in-Publication Data
Robins, Deri.
The stone in the sword / Deri and Jim Robins.—1st U.S. ed.
p.   cm.
Summary: Leofric, squire to Sir Garderobe, is led on a mad chase when the emerald falls out of his knight's sword and is carried off by a monkey.
ISBN 0-7636-0313-9
[1. Knights and knighthood—Fiction. 2. Monkeys—Fiction.] I. Robins, Jim, ill. II. Title.
PZ7.R5545St   1998
[Fic]—dc21   97-24065
2 4 6 8 10 9 7 5 3 1
Printed in Belgium
This book was typeset in Golden Type Original. The pictures were done in watercolor and ink.
Candlewick Press, 2067 Massachusetts Avenue, Cambridge, Massachusetts 02140

The Stone in the Sword

DERI AND JIM ROBINS

CANDLEWICK PRESS
CAMBRIDGE, MASSACHUSETTS

HELLO—MY NAME'S LEOFRIC! I'm squire to
Sir Garderobe of Squall Castle—although, a few years
ago my pet monkey, Barbarossa, nearly lost me my job.

It was the day before the winter jousting tournament, and I had
a huge pile of armor to clean. I was giving my master's sword a
final polish when the priceless emerald in the hilt clattered onto
the flagstones. Barbarossa grabbed it up in his hairy paw and
headed off at top speed! I followed him into the kitchen—and
that was where my problems *really* began. . . .

✦ **Join Leofric in his quest for the valuable stone
in the sword! Find out what happens to the
emerald and then follow it through the book.**

✦ **Look out for the ghost of Sir Harald Garderobe.
He was the first owner of the sword, and he has
vowed not to rest until the emerald is found.**

✦ **Melissa is the great-great-granddaughter of the
magician Merlin. Thanks to her talent for seeing into
the future, some very modern objects have slipped
into her tapestries. See if you can spot them all.**

✦ **Sir Gawhine is in love with fair Eglantine. Much to his
embarrassment, he is followed wherever he goes by Stave
the minstrel, who loves to sing about other people's business.
Pay careful attention to the words of Stave's songs.**

✦ **There are lots of other medieval mix-ups
to look out for too.**

✦ **To start looking for Barbarossa, turn the page.**

IN THE KITCHEN, everyone was even hotter and busier than usual. The castle was full of guests for the tournament, and a great feast was going on upstairs. I'd just about caught up with Barbarossa when I collided with an understeward. As we crashed to the floor, I saw Barbarossa drop the emerald. . . .

✦ **Find where the emerald has landed.**

Gawhine has written a letter to Eglantine and has paid a servant to deliver it.

✦ **Can you find the letter?**

The chief steward has told Leofric to look for all the things that are lost in the kitchen.

✦ **Can you help him?**

✦ **Can you see two modern-looking kitchen gadgets in Melissa's tapestry?**

✦ **Where is the ghost of Sir Harald?**

Oh, this is the ballad of bold Gawhine,
Who dared not speak to Eglantine;
A letter to his love he wrote. . . .
(A tasty dish does hide the note!)

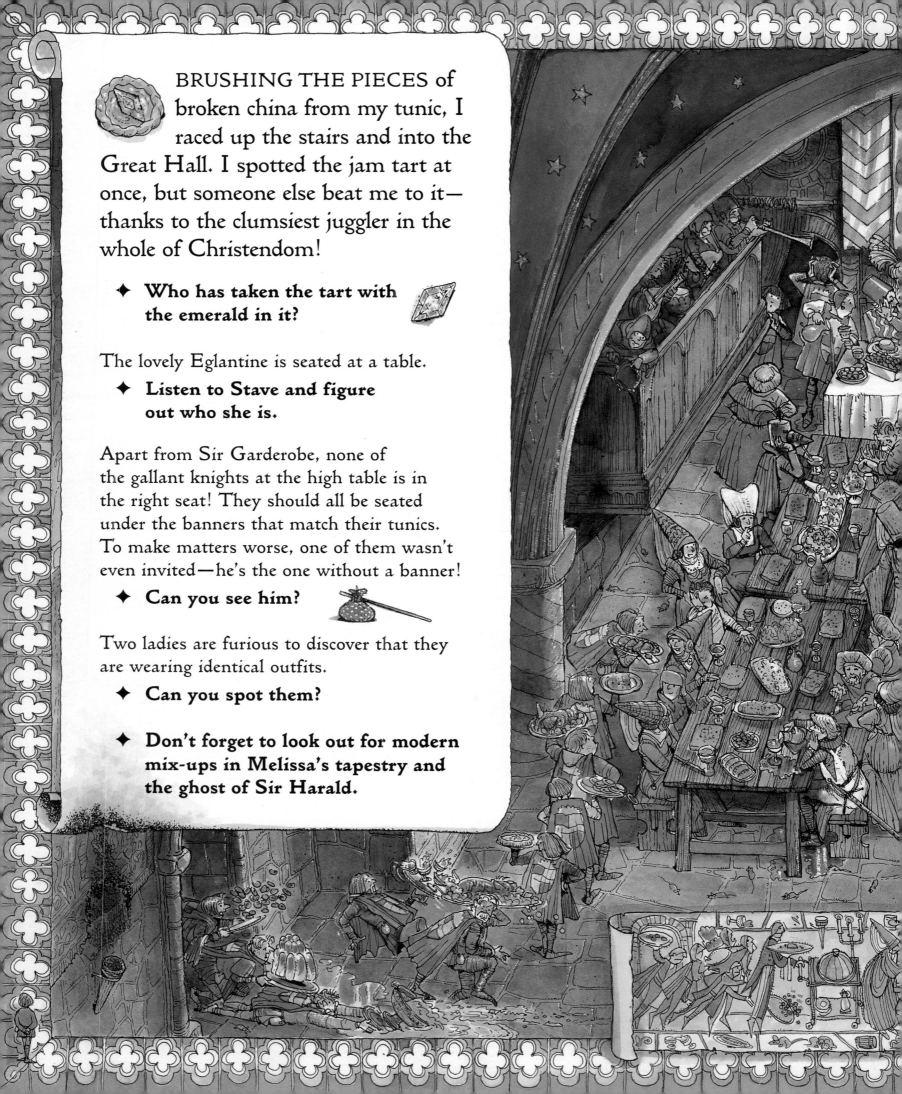

BRUSHING THE PIECES of broken china from my tunic, I raced up the stairs and into the Great Hall. I spotted the jam tart at once, but someone else beat me to it—thanks to the clumsiest juggler in the whole of Christendom!

✦ **Who has taken the tart with the emerald in it?**

The lovely Eglantine is seated at a table.

✦ **Listen to Stave and figure out who she is.**

Apart from Sir Garderobe, none of the gallant knights at the high table is in the right seat! They should all be seated under the banners that match their tunics. To make matters worse, one of them wasn't even invited—he's the one without a banner!

✦ **Can you see him?**

Two ladies are furious to discover that they are wearing identical outfits.

✦ **Can you spot them?**

✦ **Don't forget to look out for modern mix-ups in Melissa's tapestry and the ghost of Sir Harald.**

BY THE TIME I'd caught up with the knave at the castle gates, he was in the safe hands of the chief steward. But where was the tart? I looked anxiously at all the people going in and out of the castle.

✦ **Where has the knave put the tart?**

Gawhine wants to know if Eglantine will meet him in the forest (that's what the letter was about). He's asked her to answer him in a special secret code—which isn't secret anymore!

✦ **Can you read her message?**

The gardener is taking a bag of turnips to the monastery. He's hoping to get a ride with a friend who's mending a roof.

✦ **Can you see his friend?**

Egbert's mother is looking for him because he's forgotten to put on his scarf (his hat and scarf have the same pattern).

✦ **Can you help her find him?**

✦ **Don't forget Melissa's mix-ups or the ghost of Sir Harald.**

AS I PUSHED my way through the crowd, I saw the woodsman vanish into the forest. I finally tracked him down in a clearing and was just about to hail him when, to my horror, I saw that the emerald was on the move again!

✦ **Can you find the new thief?**

Sir Garderobe is fed up with outlaws poaching his pheasants, so he's sent his soldiers to arrest them. But the outlaws aren't that easy to find (especially since they always wear green).

✦ **Can you spot six outlaws?**

The outlaws won't hurt Leofric, but he needs to look out for hungry wolves.

✦ **Can you find three wolves?**

Eglantine is annoyed because Gawhine is so late.

✦ **Stave knows what's holding him up!**

A traveler is being given three sets of directions. Two of the peasants are lying.

✦ **Can you figure out who is telling the truth?**

Go straight to the crossroads, then go around the pile of logs.

No, go back the way you came, then go left at the path that goes around Lioness Rock.

Cross the bridge, then take the road that goes past the well.

Which is the path to White Church?

Gawhine did wear a cloak of red,
A feather'd cap upon his head;
('Tis no surprise a local peasant
Mistook him for a passing pheasant!)

THE LAD RACED OFF through the forest—with me in hot pursuit! By the time I caught up with him at the fair, he'd already taken a big bite out of the tart! My heart sank to my boots—then soared again, as I saw that at last the emerald was going to be in safe hands. . . .

✦ **What has Leofric seen?**

The dancers should each be sharing two ribbons with their partner. However, only the couple sharing the red and green ribbons have gotten it right.

✦ **Can you figure out who should be dancing with whom?**

✦ **Which of the two farmers has been the most successful at the fair?**

Gawhine is taking part in an archery contest, but all three of his red arrows have missed the target.

✦ **Can you see where they went?**

✦ **Can you see Eglantine? Stave knows where she is!**

Gawhine has failed to win a prize!
Scorn fills his lady's mocking eyes!
Declaring she can stand no more,
She leaves with Tom, the troubadour!

A BLIZZARD was blowing, so I sheltered for the night at the monastery of the Barefoot Brotherhood. The emerald was locked in a chest for safekeeping and Brother Francis stood guard outside the door.

Just after dawn, I was woken with the terrible news that the emerald had been stolen. I ran down the stairs and peered into the empty chest. Had I lost the stone in the sword for good?

✦ **What's happened to Brother Francis?**

It's not too late to catch the thief!

✦ **Can you figure out who he is? Which route should Leofric take to reach him? (He can go only through doors that are already open.)**

The thief has knocked the head off a statue.

✦ **Can you see where it should go?**

Gawhine has also spent the night here. He's hoping someone will clean his boots!

✦ **Do you know where he is sleeping?**

WE CHASED THE THIEF into town, where he disappeared into the crowd. I climbed a wall to get a better look, and I saw that my quest was hopeless.

✦ **Who has taken the emerald this time?**

Gawhine's decided that the life of a monk is not for him. He's hoping to see Eglantine at the market.

✦ **Stave spots her first. Can you see her?**

✦ **Help Mistress Slowly find her seven ghastly children. They're redheaded and freckled like her.**

Meg needs everything on this shopping list.

✦ **What does she still need to get, and where can she buy it?**

bread
ribbons
grapes
cheese
fish
pies

Three of the forest outlaws are in the crowd.

✦ **Can you see them?**

I TRUDGED SLOWLY back to Squall Castle. It was now the morning of the tournament and I still hadn't found the emerald. There seemed to be a lot of noise and excitement, but all I could think of was how I had failed my master. . . .

There's still hope!

◆ **Can you see the emerald?**

Some knights have just returned from their travels.

◆ **Listen to the ladies' gossip. Which knight is each one talking about?**

The chief steward is ordering the maids and butlers to serve mead and wine to the knights.

◆ **Find out how many knights drink mead and how many like wine. Who should go back to the kitchen to fetch more goblets — the maids (serving mead) or the butlers (serving wine)?**

◆ **Where's Eglantine's pet falcon? It has a ribbon that matches her gown. . . .**

Seven snakes have escaped from their basket!

◆ **Can you see them?**

You haven't any money left, Will!

I'll bet my clothes!

Pelidor says it is delicious, as long as you don't eat the skin.

Tristan's been teaching it to talk.

It doesn't *look* strong, but Godfrye plans to ride it in the tournament!

The knights of the Red Lion
like mead, but those of the
Green Dragon drink only wine.

Fair Eglantine has found a net;
She begs Gawhine to grab her pet.
She points, and cries, "It never bites!"
No use! Gawhine's afraid of heights!

WITH A HEAVY heart, I went to dress my master for the tournament. On the way, I saw that the maids had mixed up the laundry, and many people had been given the wrong-sized clothes. Suddenly, a familiar green glint caught my eye—then, just as quickly, it was gone again!

✦ **Who grabbed the emerald?**

Sir Bartizan and Sir Barbican, the castle twins, have mixed up their clothes.

✦ **Can you find the twin knights with socks that don't match?**

✦ **What has made Eglantine so angry?**

Tristan's lost his helmet!

✦ **Can you find it?**

✦ **Which portrait shows Sir Harald? He was quite young when it was painted, but he'd already grown his fine red beard.**

SHIELDING THE WINTRY sun from my eyes, I chased Barbarossa over the castle walls. Luckily, the little brute stopped to eat a bunch of bananas—but where had he tossed the emerald?

✦ **Can you find the emerald?**

Tristan needs to hurry if he's going to get to the tournament in time.

✦ **How can he get down from that turret window without breaking both legs?**

Gawhine's so nervous about his joust that he's lost his lance.

✦ **Can you find it?**

Will is freezing! He lost all his clothes playing dice!

✦ **Can you help him find something to wrap himself up in?**

I GRABBED THE emerald and dashed off to the armory to have it fixed back into the sword. I was just in time—the trumpets were blowing and the jousts were about to begin! It was a great tournament and all the knights fought bravely.

Sir Garderobe's sword is gleaming brightly—it's a pity about the rest of his armor!

✦ **Can you see him?**

Isolde has given her scarf to her favorite knight.

✦ **Who is he?**

✦ **How has Gawhine done in the tournament?**

Everyone who has handled the emerald is here.

✦ **Find them all. Who else do you recognize?**

Melissa's given up sewing. She's had a much better idea.

✦ **Can you find her?**

As for me, I was the happiest squire in all of England. Despite all that had happened, I hadn't failed my master— no thanks to Barbarossa!

THE QUEST ISN'T OVER YET!

While Leofric's been searching for the emerald, quite a lot of other things have been going on, too. How many of these did you notice?

THE ARCHER

Help him find his missing archery target, and look for him in all the other pictures, too.

TWO QUARRELING SERVANTS

It all began with some spilled soup, and things got worse and worse. Follow their quarrel through the book.

LADY ISOLDE

Lady Isolde appears in six pictures. Can you find her? She's not very fond of birds. Why might this be a problem in the future?

PERCEVAL

He'll do anything for a free lunch — which he usually tucks into his red-and-white polka-dot hankie! Find him in every picture.

LADY VERONICA

She's had her eye on Gawhine for quite a while — all the way through the book, in fact! You'll see her in all but two pictures (ladies aren't allowed into monasteries, and she never goes near the kitchen).